in the same series

Magic Water
The Christmas Box
Sam Pig and the Hurdy-Gurdy Man

The Adventures of Sam Pig

Sam Pig and his Fiddle

Alison Uttley

Illustrated by Graham Percy

Guild Publishing
LONDON

First published in 1939
by Faber and Faber Limited
3 Queen Square London WC1N 3AU
This edition first published in 1988

This edition published in 1988
by Guild Publishing
by arrangement with Faber and Faber Ltd.

CN 7469

Printed in Great Britain by
W. S. Cowell Ltd Ipswich

British Library Cataloguing in Publication Data

Uttley, Alison
Sam Pig and his fiddle. –
(The Adventures of Sam Pig).
I. Title   II. Percy, Graham
823'.912[J]   PZ7

ISBN 0–571–15162–0

Sam Pig and his Fiddle

Sister Ann Pig sat in her rocking chair one fine
morning, darning a hole in somebody's sock. As
she put her needle in and out, she sang this ditty
in a little squeaky voice:

'There once was a young little, fat little, pig
Not very old, and not very big.
He used to be lazy, but now he must dig!
Hey Ho!
Hey Ho!
This fat little lazy pig!'

Little Sam Pig lolled against the doorpost, chewing a straw, but when he heard Ann's song he pricked up his ears.

'Does she mean me?' he asked himself. 'She cannot mean me! Why, I am the youngest of the family. Surely Sister Ann doesn't want me to do any work?'

He peeped round the corner, but Ann's eyes were glued to the big hole in the heel of her sock. She threaded her needle and then sang another verse in her shrill treble.

'He must plant the potato and gather the fig,
Take up a spade and dig and dig,
Then I'll give him a fiddle to play me a jig,
Hey Ho!
Hey Ho!
This fat little lazy pig!

Sam threw away his straw, coughed loudly, and entered the room.

'I met a brown rabbit down the lane,' said he, 'and he was so sorry for me, tears came to his eyes as he looked at me.'

'Why? What's the matter with you?' asked Ann, putting down the sock and half rising.

'He said I had grown so thin!' sighed Sam, and he stroked his stout body with a dejected air.

'Really, Sam!' laughed Ann, dropping back to her seat. 'Really! You are like a roly-poly pudding, or an apple dumpling. You are far too lazy. Once you used to help us, but now you do nothing but lounge in doorways. Take a spade and dig.'

'Ann, did you mean me in that song of a fat little pig?'

'If the cap fits, wear it,' said Ann.

'Then,' said Sam triumphantly, 'give me a fiddle to play you a jig.'

'Certainly, when you've planted the potatoes and helped poor Brother Bill. He does all the gardening nowadays.'

Sam sighed and went to the garden. There was Bill digging away in the potato patch, putting stones in one basket, and weeds in another, and the worms in another. It looked quite fun, and besides, Sam was really tired of doing nothing, so he took up a spade and began to dig as hard as he could.

By the time Tom Pig had cooked the dinner and Ann had darned the stockings, the potato patch was finished, and Sam was decidedly thinner

'Am I thin enough to have a fiddle?' he asked.

'Not quite,' replied Ann. 'You must work a little longer.' So each day Sam dug so hard that the pile of stones he took from the soil was big enough to build a house, and the weeds made a haystack. Bill made a kennel with the stones and invited a stray and homeless hedgehog to live

there, to keep watch and ward in return for free lodging and a bowl of milk each day.

'Is it time for me to have a fiddle?' asked Sam.

'Not yet. There are seeds to be sown, and beans to be planted. We must have a good crop this year; we shall need it.' Ann tapped the barometer, sniffed the air, and shook her head.

Sam and Bill planted little brown potatoes in deep trenches, and covered them with earth, clean and fresh with never a stone or weed. They made rows of tiny holes and popped speckledy beans into them. They planted young cabbages and cauliflowers in neat beds of rich loam. They sowed the seeds of radishes, carrots, cress, lettuce, and parsley.

'Is it time for me to have a fiddle, Sister Ann?'

asked Sam at the end of the week. All his fat
flabbiness was gone, and he was strong and happy.

'No, not yet,' replied Ann. 'There is watering,
hoeing, raking to be done. Slugs must be caught,
and caterpillars trapped, and centipedes sent about
their business.'

That night Badger came to see his young
friends. He stroked the hedgehog and gave it a
green bone. The hedgehog gratefully shook its

prickles. All the pigs hurried to get Badger's bedroom ready. Ann put clean sheets on the bed, Sam fetched his carpet slippers. Tom made an omelette with twenty eggs, and Bill swept the yard and polished the door-scraper.

'Is all well?' asked Badger as he sank slowly into his big armchair which was always kept ready for him, and stretched out his short legs with a sigh of content. 'Is all well?'

'Yes, Badger,' said Ann, meekly.

'Is there a good crop sown in the garden?' continued the Badger.

'Yes,' nodded Ann. 'Sam and Bill have worked hard.'

'All the better for them. You will need it. I have heard something down in the ground. I've had a message from the air. The swallows brought it. This will be a remarkable summer!'

He sat silent, and the pigs crept softly to wash up the supper things. The sun had set. The blackbirds were calling 'Good-night. Good-night' in the hedgerow, and the rooks were returning to their homes in the elms. It was time for bed.

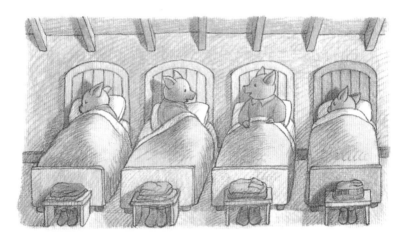

The next morning when the family awoke, Badger had gone. Nothing but an empty larder told them that he had visited them.

'He's always like that,' sighed Ann. 'We do love him so much, but he's here today and gone tomorrow.'

'Here yesterday and gone today,' sighed Bill.

'Here at sunset and gone at sunrise,' sighed Tom.

'Here never, and gone forever,' sighed Sam.

The pigs worked in their garden, obedient to Badger's last words, and the vegetables and flowers

flourished as they had never done before. Every day the sun shone, but never a drop of rain fell from the blue sky, so they hoed the ground, and kept it moist, and watered it from the brook.

One bright morning Ann went to market, and Sam waited at home with a hope in his heart. Would she remember her promise? She brought

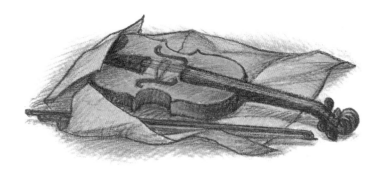

back her string bag bursting with good things, muffins, pop-corn, and gingerbread pigs. In a parcel under her arm was a fiddle, wrapped carefully in brown paper. It was just such a fiddle as a slim little pig would like, a nice reddish one, with two fine curly holes in which he could keep his handkerchief, his marbles and bits and bobs. There was a little bridge holding the strings, and a long hairy bow. When Sam touched the strings they sang such a tune, he fairly squealed with excitement.

He danced up and down, and plucked the strings, for he hadn't time to use the bow. He played 'Wigs on the Green', and 'John, John, The Grey Goose is Gone', until Ann covered her ears.

Every night Sam Pig played his fiddle and the others sang in their high shrill voices the old piggy folk-songs which have long been forgotten. Every night the stars shone down on the four small pigs sitting in the doorway, with Sam in the middle, playing and singing to the bats and swallows, which dipped low to listen and piped in answer.

Summer had come and every day grew hotter. No animal could remember such blazing days. The pigs tended their garden, and the onions and carrots, the peas and beans grew like a forest of food. In the fields the sun had burnt up the good grass and withered the salads under the hedges and dried the rootcrops

Little noses pressed against the gate as animals passed on their way to market. Little sad faces looked in between the bars as they returned with empty baskets. The stalls at the fair had nothing on them except husks and dry beans, and the animals went hungry to bed.

'Let's invite them all in,' said Ann. 'I think that was what Badger intended us to do.'

'Yes, let's,' said Tom. 'I'll fill their baskets with lots of green vegetables and rosy fruit.'

'Yes, let's,' said Bill, 'and I'll give them mugs of cool water from our deep spring, for the stream is dry in the meadow.'

'Yes, let's,' squeaked Sam. 'I'll play them some cheerful tunes on my fiddle.'

So Ann threw open the gate. 'Come in. Come in!' she called. 'Here is plenty! Come and feast!'

The animals poured in – the brown rabbits, with their soft gentle glances, the shy hares, the quick-moving red squirrels, the field-mice, the water-rats, and the hedgehogs. Little hedgehog in the tiny house was so excited to see some relations that he rushed out to meet them. He said he wouldn't change his nice kennel, 'No, not for all the gold in the Indies,' whatever that meant.

Tom filled the small woven baskets with peas and cabbage leaves, with radishes and lettuces. Bill fetched mugs of pure cold water from the well, and Ann made camomile tea in her best silver tea-pot for the older animals, while Sam played amusing jigs and dances to entertain the youngest creatures.

Away down the lane trotted the happy rabbits, the merry squirrels, the tall hares and waddling ducks, the handsome water-rats, and gay little field-mice, the solemn hedgehogs and sleek moles. They had been invited to come again the next day, and each day as long as the drought lasted, for there was plenty of food for every one.

Sam sat on a tree stump, and sang another song
to a few young animals who wanted to stay a little
while longer. There are always some who don't
want to go home when the time comes.

There once was a young little slim little ME,
Who planted potatoes and gathered the pea,
Who fed the poor rabbits and gave them some tea.
Hey Ho! That slim little ME!

He played on his fiddle, tim-tiddle-dee-dee,
He worked as hard as the busiest bee,
His garden was lovely as lovely can be!
Hey Ho! That slim little ME!'

'Oh Sam!' cried Sister Ann, when she heard him. 'Little boasting Sam! Off to bed at once!' and Sam scurried upstairs with the fiddle under his arm, and the young animals ran away home.